For Port Hope (the inspiration for
this story) and, of course, for Guido.
— PS

To my future dog … who inspired
me throughout this book.
— ND

Text copyright © 2021 by Patricia Storms
Illustrations copyright © 2021 by Nathalie Dion
Published in Canada and the USA in 2021 by Groundwood Books

All rights reserved. No part of this publication may be reproduced, stored in a retrieval system or transmitted, in any form or by any means, without the prior written consent of the publisher or a license from The Canadian Copyright Licensing Agency (Access Copyright). For an Access Copyright license, visit www.accesscopyright.ca or call toll free to 1-800-893-5777.

Groundwood Books / House of Anansi Press
groundwoodbooks.com

We gratefully acknowledge for their financial support of our publishing program the Canada Council for the Arts, the Ontario Arts Council and the Government of Canada.

Groundwood Books respectfully acknowledges that the land on which we operate is the Traditional Territory of many Nations, including the Anishinabeg, the Wendat and the Haudenosaunee. It is also the Treaty Lands of the Mississaugas of the Credit.

Library and Archives Canada Cataloguing in Publication
Title: The dog's gardener / Patricia Storms ; pictures by Nathalie Dion.
Names: Storms, Patricia, author. | Dion, Nathalie, illustrator.
Identifiers: Canadiana (print) 20200299069 | Canadiana (ebook) 20200299492 | ISBN 9781773062563 (hardcover) | ISBN 9781773062570 (EPUB) | ISBN 9781773065175 (Kindle)
Classification: LCC PS8637.T6755 D64 2021 | DDC jC813/.6—dc23

The illustrations consist of hand-painted gouache textures combined with painting using a digital pastel brush.
Design by Michael Solomon
Printed and bound in Malaysia

Canada Council
for the Arts
Conseil des Arts
du Canada

ONTARIO ARTS COUNCIL
CONSEIL DES ARTS DE L'ONTARIO
an Ontario government agency
un organisme du gouvernement de l'Ontario

With the participation of the Government of Canada
Avec la participation du gouvernement du Canada | Canada

MIX
Paper from
responsible sources
FSC® C012700

THE
DOG'S
GARDENER

WORDS BY
PATRICIA STORMS

PICTURES BY
NATHALIE DION

Groundwood Books
House of Anansi Press
Toronto / Berkeley

I can hear her soft step on the
stairs. She doesn't know I'm awake.
I always pretend to be asleep, just
so I can hear her gentle voice.

"Time to get up, Dutch."

Then I wait for those
beautiful words.

"Okay, Dutch. Let's go outside."

It's the bright time of year.

The little house frightens me. It's dark
and dusty and full of sharp things.
But she needs what's inside.

While she works, I roll in the dewy grass and breathe in the sweet, rich smells around me.

Today she's making new holes in the ground.
I sniff in approval, but truthfully I am waiting
for her warm hand to scratch my ears.

It's very bright now. Soon she'll walk
to the great stump for her midday rest.

She sits very still, and I nap peacefully on her boots. But only for a short time.

"Okay, Dutch. Back we go."

From up here I see the beauty of all her work.
Oh joy! She's bringing out the water.

The light is starting to dim.

She's finishing up. Soon she'll call for
me, and we'll walk back home ...

together.